To Ella, Elijah, Asher, and River.
From your breath, I have seen galaxies.
—D.F.

For Susan: Your breath is wasted on the world;
you should breathe only into other lungs.
—B.R.

Text copyright © 2020 Diana Farid
Illustrations copyright © 2020 Billy Renkl

Book design by Melissa Nelson Greenberg

Library of Congress Cataloging-in-Publication Data available.
ISBN: 978-1-944903-93-0

Printed in China

10 9 8 7 6 5 4 3 2 1

Cameron Kids is an imprint of Cameron + Company

Cameron + Company
Petaluma, California
www.cameronbooks.com

WHEN YOU BREATHE

written by DIANA FARID
illustrated by BILLY RENKL

cameron kids

Tree leaves sway
when it flows by.

Birds need it
to flutter and fly.

It carries your favorite song,
stirs with stardust—
the grand atoms of the universe.

When you breathe—
whoosh!—

breath fills
the upside-down tree
inside your rising chest.

Breath wisps
through the tree trunk
and its white bark.

It reaches deeper,
rushes into branches
bound for the tree's canopy.

Breath blooms
at tree tips,
like sprouting leaves
on lush spring stems.

Then,
those grand atoms,
which make the stars,
burst across
millions of marvelous buds.

It just takes seconds
for a piece of the sky
to fill your heart.

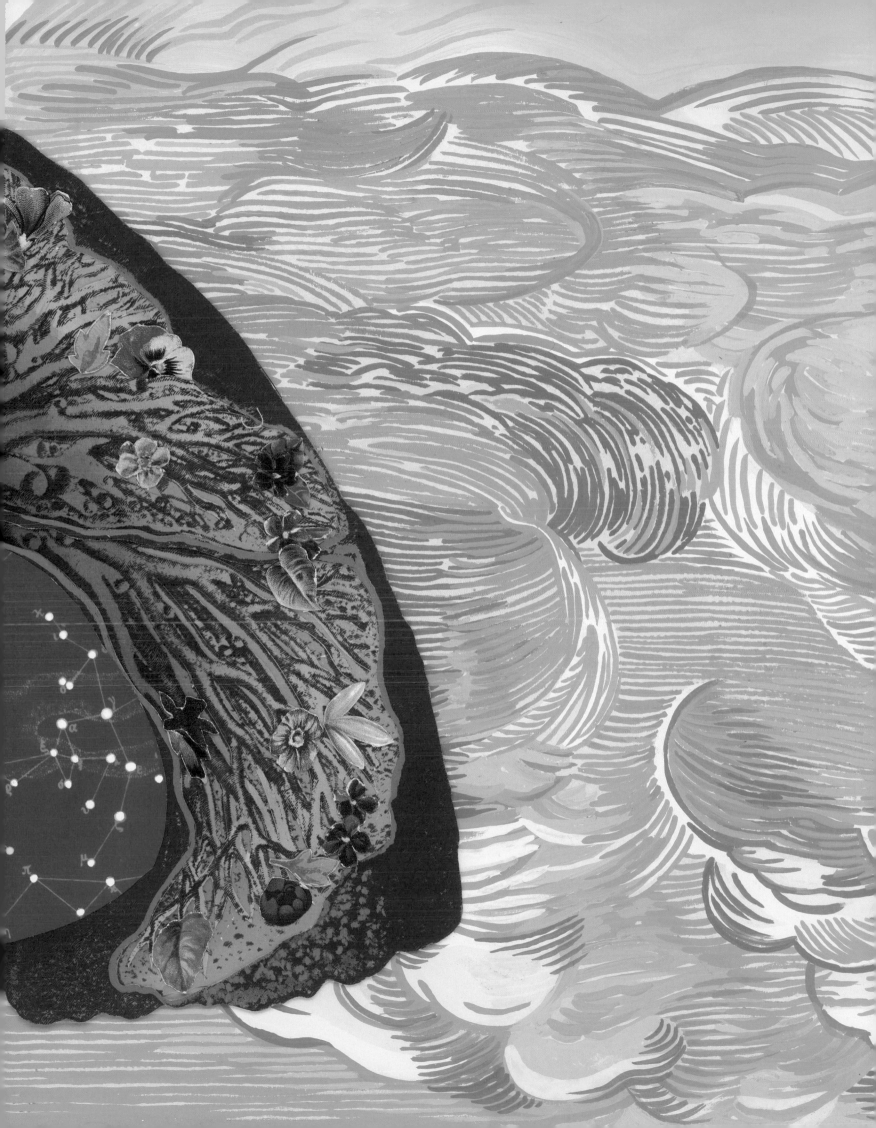

When you breathe,
breath sparks,

every step,
every hop,
every ascending tune.

You are light.

When you breathe out, exhale,
your breath returns
back to the breeze,
becomes air again.

Air vibrates chords,
lifts up your voice,
and soars.

Above the tree leaves,
beyond the birds,
stardust sparkles in your song.

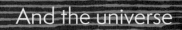

And the universe   rings with it.

Air.
Breath.

You.

BREATHING WORDS

Inhale: When we inhale, we take in a breath. We do this about 12 to 20 times every minute.

Atoms: Atoms are the small pieces of the world around us. Some examples of atoms in the air we breathe are carbon, nitrogen, and oxygen.

Carbon: Carbon is in everything that is alive and is one of the important atoms that we breathe out.

Nitrogen: Nitrogen atoms make up most of the air on Earth.

Oxygen: Oxygen makes up about one-fifth of the air on Earth. Plants, animals, and people need oxygen to live. Oxygen gives us energy.

Brain: The brain is the part of the body in the head that receives information from all body parts and sends out messages to all body parts. The brain controls our breathing.

Energy: Energy gives us the power to do the things we want to do. Our bodies get energy from air, food, and sleeping.

Muscles: Muscles are made up of bunches of special cells that are able to squeeze themselves smaller, helping body parts move.

Diaphragm: The diaphragm is an important breathing muscle that spans across the bottom of the thorax and separates it from the lower parts in the belly, also called the abdomen. When we inhale, the diaphragm pulls down.

Ribs: The ribs are curved bones that surround our lungs.

Intercostal muscles: The intercostal muscles connect the ribs and help them to move.

Thorax: The thorax is the part of the body between the neck and the diaphragm. Sometimes, the thorax is called the chest. The lungs are in the thorax, under the ribs. When we breathe, ribs and muscles help the thorax expand to make more room for our breath.

Lungs: The air that we breathe goes into the lungs. There is a right lung and a left lung.

Trachea: The trachea is a tube that carries air from the nose and mouth down to the lungs. Part of the trachea is made up of 16 to 20 hard rings.

Cartilage: The rings of the trachea are made of cartilage. Cartilage is strong and flexible. It has a white hue.

Cilia: Cilia are tiny, moving hairlike structures. The inside of the trachea is lined with cilia that help keep the bronchi clean.

Bronchi: Bronchi are tubes that branch off of the trachea and carry air deeper into the lungs.

Bronchioles: The bronchioles are the smallest air-carrying tubes of the lungs.

Alveoli: Alveoli are the small pockets at the very deepest part of the lungs where atoms that make up the air, like oxygen, move across thin walls and into the blood.

Red blood cells: Red blood cells are the parts of blood that collect oxygen from the alveoli and deliver it to the rest of the body.

Heart: The heart is a hollow muscle in the middle of the chest that pumps blood. Each heartbeat helps red blood cells move, from just next to the alveoli to all our body parts that need energy.

Larynx: The larynx is in the back of the mouth and just above the trachea. Muscles in the larynx help move special strings, called the vocal chords. As air rushes by the vocal chords, they vibrate to help us make different sounds, including our own voices.

Exhale: When we exhale, we breathe air out through the nose or mouth. Our bodies do this about 12 to 20 times a minute.